Car
Wars

Tom Easton and Sophie Escabasse

WAYLAND
www.waylandbooks.co.uk

Miss Collins is the Careers Officer. She's been fixing up work experience for me. She gave me a card with a job on it.

"Don't mess this up, Dan,"
Miss Collins said.

The jobs I've tried so far haven't
gone well. But it wasn't my fault.
Not always anyway.

My heart sank as I read the card. "Used car sales?" I said. "I'd rather work at the Rubbish Tip than do this."

"Imran took that job," said Miss Collins.
"Lucky old Imran," I said. "Used car
sales it is then."

The man at the car yard
was called Fred.
Fred looked beefy.

I thought Fred would make me clean the cars. But he said, "Sell as many cars as you can."

He clapped me on the shoulder.
It nearly knocked me over.
  "The price labels are just
a guide," Fred said. "You can
do a deal with the buyer."

"Nothing here is worth more than £1,000. If you can get £2,000 then you're doing really well," Fred said. "The car keys are all in the office."

"Which cars can I sell?" I asked.

"All of them," he boomed.

"Everything is for sale!"

Then he walked away.

12

The car yard was huge.
All the cars had a price label.

I walked around the car yard.
A few people were looking
at the cars. No-one seemed to
want to buy.

I didn't blame them. The cars were rusty. One car had some squirrels living in it.

![Freestylers]

"How much for that car?" a man said.

He pointed to a red sports car.

It was parked at the front of the yard.

"Isn't there a price label on it?"
I asked.

"No," the man said. "That's why
I'm asking."

I tried to remember what Fred had told me. Nothing was worth more than £1000. Try and get £2000.

"Err, £2000?" I said.

The man stared at me. He looked surprised.

"£2000?" he said. "For that?"

"£1500?" I said.

"Are you serious?" he asked.

"Okay," I said. "£1000, but I can't go any lower." The man gave me a look.

I played it cool and waited.

"You've got a deal," he said.
The man wrote out a cheque
quickly.

"Yes!" I thought.

"I'll get the keys from the office,"
I said.

"No need," the man said. "They
are in the ignition."

"Oh, OK," I said. "Well off you go, then."

The man drove off quickly. He didn't look back.

23

Fred came back.

I was grinning from ear to ear.

"I sold a car!" I said.

"Brilliant!" he replied. He didn't look at me. He seemed to be looking for something.

"I got £1,000," I said.

"Not bad," he said. He was still looking about.

"What are you looking for?" I asked.

"I thought I parked my car here," Fred said. "A red sports car."

My stomach did a flip.

"Ah," I said. "Was that your car?"

"Yes," he said.

"*Now* you tell me," I said.

"Where's my car?" demanded Fred.
His face was like thunder.

"Well, you did say *everything*
is for sale…" I said.

I don't think I'm very good
at selling cars. But I am
good at running.

Read more stories about Dan.

Dan's latest work experience is as a grave digger. All Dan has to do is dig a hole. What could possibly go wrong?

978 0 7502 8225 3

Dan's latest work experience is at a flower shop. All Dan has to do is deliver flowers on Valentine's Day. What could possibly go wrong?

978 0 7502 8226 0

Dan's latest work experience is at a radio station. All Dan has to do is mop floors. What could possibly go wrong?

978 0 7502 8227 7

Read some more books in the Freestylers series.

FOOTBALL FACTOR

Each story follows the ups and downs of one member of the football team Sheldon Rovers as they aim for Cup glory.

978 0 7502 7985 7

978 0 7502 7980 2

978 0 7502 7982 6

978 0 7502 7984 0

978 0 7502 7981 9

978 0 7502 7983 3

SHORT THRILLERS

Cool crime detectives, Jas and Sam, solve spine-chilling cases with humour and bravery.

978 0 7502 6895 0

978 0 7502 6896 7

978 0 7502 6898 1

978 0 7502 6897 4

FOR TEACHERS

About Freestylers

Freestylers is a series of carefully levelled stories, especially geared for struggling readers. With very low reading age and high interest age, these books are humorous, fun, up-to-the-minute and edgy. Core characters provide familiarity in all of the stories, build confidence and ease pupils from one story through to the next, accelerating reading progress.

Freestylers can be used for both guided and independent reading. To make the most of the books you can:

- Focus on making each reading session successful. Talk about the text before the pupil starts reading. Introduce the characters, the storyline and any unfamiliar vocabulary.

- Encourage the pupil to talk about the book during reading and after reading. How would they have felt if they were one of the characters? How would they have dealt with the situations that Dan found himself in?

- Talk about which parts of the story they like best and why.

For guidance, this story has been approximately measured to:

National Curriculum Level: 2B
Reading Age: 6
Book Band: Orange

ATOS: 2.5
Lexile ® Measure [confirmed]: 200L